W9-CEJ-090

FOR ISABEL CAMPBELL

Clarion Books
a Houghton Mifflin Company imprint
215 Park Avenue South, New York, NY 10003
Copyright © 1981 by Dick Gackenbach

*Library of Congress Cataloging in Publication Data*

Gackenbach, Dick.    A bag full of pups.
Summary: Most of the people who take one of the 12 pups
Mr. Mullin is giving away want a dog to perform some sort of task
for them, but the little boy just wants a pet to love.
[1. Dogs—Fiction]   I. Title.
PZ7.G117 Bag    [E]    80-23230    ISBN 0-395-30081-9

PA  ISBN  0-89919-179-7
**WOZ** 10  9

# A Bag Full of Pups

## By Dick Gackenbach

CLARION BOOKS

NEW YORK

Mr. Mullin's old dog had a litter of twelve pups. "I must find a home for them," said Mr. Mullin. Early one morning, he put the pups in a bag and went to town.

"Puppies!" Mr. Mullin cried.
"Free pups! Who wants a pup?"

"I want a pup," said a Farmer.
"He will help me herd my cows."

"I will take two pups,"
said a Magician. "They
will learn to do tricks
on the stage."

"I need a pup," said
a Blind Man. "I will
train her to guide me
when I walk."

"I want a pup," said a Lady.
"I will dress him in fancy hats,
and coats, and little boots."

"I want a pup," said
a Fireman. "She will ride
in the Fire Truck with me."

"I will take a pup," said
a Policewoman. "He will
help me catch the bad guys."

"I want a pup," said a lady
who was hard of hearing.
"He will tell me when
someone knocks on my door."

"I will take a pup," said
a Grocer. "She will keep the
rats away from my cheese."

"I want a pup," said
a Dog Trainer. "I will
train him to win ribbons
and prizes."

"I want a pup," said a Hunter.
"He will go hunting with me."

At the end of the day,
one pup was still in the bag.
"I don't think anyone wants you,"
said Mr. Mullin.
Just then a small boy came by.

"I want a pup," the boy said.
"I want a pup to play with,
  and to be my friend."
"My, that's what I call a
  lucky pup," said Mr. Mullin.